SAGA *of a* CRACK ADDICT

Spellman Bernard Smith, Jr. AKA Sir Dog

Copyright © 2019 Spellman Bernard Smith, Jr. AKA Sir Dog
All rights reserved
First Edition

PAGE PUBLISHING, INC.
New York, NY

First originally published by Page Publishing, Inc. 2019

ISBN 978-1-68456-506-1 (Paperback)
ISBN 978-1-68456-507-8 (Digital)

Printed in the United States of America

Prelude

Back in the day, I was a very successful small-time pot dealer. That was during the time when the top price I paid was $200 a pound. At that time, my house was a smoker's delight and den of sexual wonderment. One could come to my house at any time and score a dime, a lid, or ounce of weed; set down to a game of chess or go to the back bedroom and enjoy moments of sexual explorations. There was a house rule that stated, all the females must be prepared to give up *a shot of body* if she wanted to come into the house. I was the houseman; therefore, the house was mine to do or not to do. Since most of the women were younger than I was, I chose to take them on. Weed was the drug of choice along with some wine. Every once in a while, we would drop some 357s', micro dot, or various other kinds of acid. We also had the smoker's delight—wacky weed. Bernard's house was the place to go if you wanted to party. Party time could be any hour of the day. All were welcome. The only hard-and-fast rule was that you do not disturb his wife during the weekdays because she had to work. My daily use of smoke lasted for a number of years, all the way up to the years of penitentiary life.

Oh yes! I went to penitentiary on a number of charges: conspiracy to commit bank robbery, armed robbery, abduction, possession of a sawed-off shotgun, and auto theft. I was initially sentenced to a total of forty-two years. Eventually, the sentence was reduced to twenty-six years. But I carried my weed business with me to the state penitentiary. Yes! While in the "big house" I established connections that provided me with weed on a regular basis. Although I was in the state prison I had contacts that provided me with a regular supply of weed. As far as weed was concerned, nothing changed in my life. When it didn't come through the mail, it came in during visiting days. There was an officer who would bring me bags when my other contacts didn't work. I was the weed man. While there were other cons who dealt another drugs, my program was the most consistent. We would occasionally exchange products. If I wanted to snort something, and they wanted to smoke something we just swapped out. Then I was transferred from the *wall* to a trailer camp, and my business went with me. My contacts were basically the same. I even had an employee who brought me an ounce every Wednesday. Sent by my woman. He did this because he wanted to hit her daughter. They toyed with him enough that he gladly brought the bag to me.

It was while I was at the camp that we saw on TV the story where this entertainer set himself on fire while "free basing." That within itself was a turnoff. But when we heard once he was out of the hospital, he returned to free basing drug. Wow! Whatever this was, it must be good! It was at that time that I became interested in that drug. I was curious enough to want to try it. And said I was going to do so as soon as I got home. After serving six years, I was paroled. Frankly speaking, at that time free basing was far from my mind. Yet the opportunity to do so soon became real. The people I knew was doing it. And…as if it was yesterday, I remember my first hit. I was guided through the process, step-by-step by a pro.

First of all, I was impressed by the process. Red had a small leather bag that I called a kit. In it were the tools of the trade—a glass tube in which he put the cocaine and some baking soda in, and then he mixed that with some water which was in another small bottle. He then fired up a small torch with a lighter, which also was in the kit. He put the fire to the tube and the substance began to bubble up. He added some water and ice chips to it, shook it up and twirled the tube around; after a while, the stuff hardened up. In a few moments, he rolled the rock out of the tube onto the table. He took a razor, which also was in the bag, cut off a piece of the rock and put it on the pipe. He then told me to take a deep breath, blow it out completely. He then put the pipe to my mouth and put the fire to the pipe and told me to pull slowly, but not to inhale. "Slowly, pull it slowly!" "Now let it out." When I did this, I found myself floating into pace where the astronauts went! I declared, I floated above the floor! It was like nothing I'd ever experienced!

There was a woman sitting on the sofa, and instantly, I wanted a shot of that stuff. I asked her would she come into the hallway so I could talk with her. She came into the hallway. She asked me if this was my first time hitting. I told her yes. She asked me if I was trying to get with her. Yes! She then explained to me what I was going through. First she told me to feel my joint. Well, I tried. There was nothing there. It had shrunken back up in somewhere! It was then that I found that what we feel we can do, is not what we can do when we take that hit. Now this not to say that this is what happens to all of us, all the time, but for the most part, what you feel to do isn't what you can do. Simply speaking, the hit prevented the dick from rising to the occasion.

The feeling was so good I had to try another hit. After that second hit, I left and went home. I had to tell my woman what I had experienced. I told her the hit was so good that I didn't want to do it again…or so I thought…

One thing I discovered early on in that experimental stage is that I never got enough. No matter how many hits I got, it was never enough. What that revealed to me was a clear understanding of what motivated that entertainer to go back to that concoction that set him afire, and that drew him back to using.

This process is called "free basing." It was later renamed "crack." That name was given by the sound it made once the fire was put to it, that *cracking sound* like wood burning! Early on in the game we brought it by quarters twenty-five dollars or fifty dollars (fifties) pieces. And before we bought it in rock form, we bought it as powder. This was primarily snorted. In the beginning we had to get someone to cook it for us, everybody didn't know how to cook, Red didn't. But as time went on we learned to cook for ourselves. If you didn't learn how to cook your own shit, others who did it for you would usually *beat* you, and there were so many ways to beat you. My woman was a master at doing that. Hell! She would do it in your face while you watched her cook your stuff up for you. For a long time, I was one of those who couldn't cook my own rock. Therefore, I was beat out of a lot of cocaine, but thanks to the women in my life; I learned to cook. At first, there was a number of trial and error before I perfected the art of cooking.

As I said previously, there was a time when I backed away from it. That high-flying world of narcotic interludes was a bit too much. I had regulated myself to snorting powder and smoking weed and, once in a while, sipping a little drink. All was well. I was able to indulge in my favorite activities, which includes sexual interludes. Actually, snorting powder and smoking weed was the best thing going for me. As I said, the weed and powder were the catalyst that propelled me to those episodes where I was able to dance among the stars while pumping deeply within the dark recesses of some broad's fat ass.

I know of some guys who used to envy me because of my sexual prowess. That's why one of the names I had was "freak show." I was the master of freaking. At any time, I could put together an orgy. There usually was no cover charge, but one should bring a bottle or bag to show their gratitude. Plus, it would help them get through the door. Long before my shows that included rocks, there were my shows with weed and drinks. Of course, there was stuff to eat, besides bodies. Weed demanded food. When the program changed over to rock, there was no real desire for food. That was another of the major difference in the drugs. With weed we ate food. With rock we went on the stem fast diet. Though I stopped doing crack, habitually, I did dab in the crack program occasionally. But I had not been bitten by the bug of habit. The crossover moment came upon me on October 3, 1988. That was the day that I would go down in infamy. How? You might ask. Well, let me tell you my story…

During that time, my life was one that I was proud of. We had moved down to the Willoughby section of Ocean View. My wife was working on the base, and I was doing well in my photography work in the clubs. It was a wonderful arrangement. When she worked days, I was a house husband with two lovely babies to take care of during the day. Then, I would go to work at the clubs at night. I also had jobs elsewhere, doing weddings, parties. This story of mine is complex and baffling. Let me try to lay this out to you…

SAGA OF A CRACK ADDICT

A friend of my friend made me an offer, he was a hustler who recognized me as one too and wanted to help me out. He started off by extending me a helping hand by fronting me a quarter ounce of cocaine and I was to give him $300. That was a good deal because the stuff was good. In fact, it was better than what we had around the way. I had five customers, four gay guys, and one broad. I didn't need or want anymore. This was before I took on that other customer unexpectedly. It began when one of the gays asked me if I could cook it for them. They said that would help them to get over on their johns better. I told them I didn't know how to do it.

When he left, my wife said, "I do."

I said, "Do what?"

She said, "I can cook."

That floored me. But I said, "Okay."

She told me to go down to the store and get some bake and El Producto Queen Cigars. When I got back to the crib I heard her in the bathroom empting out a pill bottle. When she came into the dining room she asked me about opening up a bag, "Which one?" Told her to get a fifty. Then the show began to happen.

I watched as she wrapped some aluminum foil around the pill bottle. Tighten it on with a rubber band, took a pin and punched some holes through it. Sat it aside and took some powder and put it in the cigar tube along with some bake. (It's reminding me of Red.) After putting a little water in it the tube, she fired it up. I watched as it bubbled up. She shook it around a little and then shouted for me to get some ice. I got a cube and broke it up. She cracked it up in chips and dropped it in the tube. I watched it turn into a pearl. She then rolled it out along the tabletop, then she got some cigarette ashes and put them on the top of the pill bottled. Oh! But before she did that, she punched a hole in the side of the bottle and put a straw through it and secured it with some tape.

As she put the chip on the ashes, she instructed me to pull it slowly, not to inhale it and let it out slowly. (Again, reminding me of Red.) I did as I told and found myself again floating across the ceiling… This, indeed, was the beginning of the end. My friends that was the third of October 1988.

SPELLMAN BERNARD SMITH, JR. AKA SIR DOG

When the guy came back to get his money, he also asked me if wanted to purchase some. Because as he said, I should have had money enough to get something. What he did was to first give me some real talk and then gave me thirty grams to work with. I had to give him $1,200 in return. Couldn't ask for a better deal. He told me that whatever I was doing to stop. And to work the shot. Thus, the saga of a crack addict actually begins. My story is long and full of adventures. It has more twist and turns than a hillside mountain road in Sweden. With that thirty grams of fish scale cocaine I could have launched a program on the road to small-time riches. Instead I launched a trip to a personal hell!

My wife and I entered into the mad, mad world of rock stars. We thought we could both sell and smoke cocaine and be successful in both worlds. Ha! Though I still had the five customers I started out with, I soon became my best customer. Before too long, my wife could no longer keep working. Though I worked primarily in clubs where there were plenty of customers, slowly I began to eat up my sales. I would carry two to $300 worth of product to work with me. Yes, I sold some, but I started to out use my sale. Sale one, smoke two, not good percentage. Then I started smoking out of my home. I sold furniture piece by piece. The children's furniture and play things. Our ultraslick dinette set. I stop paying on the living-room set. I sold everything I could.

Next went the unpaid rent. Then the other rentals were slipped from under our feet. But I still said I could pull us out of the hole, which hole? I lived in a world full of holes. The major problem we had was the fact that we had two babies, a two-year-old boy and a daughter who was just a few months old. Then I let one of the gay guys to move in with us to help me with the house and children while my wife went to work, just before the work ended. Then he and I dipped into the bags.

The first time we moved out of our apartment we moved into a hotel room. Although we could afford a month's rent, it couldn't be done for long. The habit was eating us up. One of the things that was made clear to us is that if the two of us did drugs, it meant that the downfall was twice as fast.

SAGA OF A CRACK ADDICT

At one point, we had three rides. A van and two cars. The van died on the way back to the car lot, and it had to be hauled away. One of the cars was driven to my daughter's house and reportedly died in the driveway. Yet at this point in time, I still don't know what happened to the other car. In fact, I can't remember what it was. But what I can remember are the images or faces of a number of freaks who crossed my path, who dived onto my bed or those who did their very best to "raise the dead." This meant causing my dick to rise. As I said earlier, hitting the rock and hitting the pussy didn't go hand and hand. But after a while the adverse effect it has on a hard-on subsided, somewhat. The desire to engage in sex after a hit was the same, each time you got a good blast. In my world of drugs, sex, played a major role. Sex is money, and money is sex, and the rock equaled both of them. With a rock you're able to get Samika and Rahim and their brother and sisters to do anything sexual you could imagine. Fellatio or cunnilingus activity in my world was common thing to do. Most guys like having it done to them. Lots of guys like doing whatever to whomever. (Think about it!) Females rather perform fellatio than intercourse, doing it with expertise is a female's game. Frankly speaking, I mastered the fine art of love making in any and all kind of sexual undertaking. Time and time again I would engage with guys, who a very few people knew of their sexual proclivities.

At one point in my drug life, I did some wacky weed and various pills. Each of them caused me to hallucinate to some degree, but none of it sent me catapulting to outer limits of the atmosphere as crack did. It stands to reason that anything that'll cause you to soar to the height of dimensions in our world can surely compel you to reach further in the world of sexual pleasures. I remember that I said the first time I took a hit. I took off like an astronaut in a spaceship going to outer space. The only thing that equals it is the combination of coke and cock/cunt. Each costing tons of money. And the only way to minimize the cost is through trading. Simply put, the girls give up the hot lips, or the deep hot, juicy, honey pot in one fashion or the other. The guy lays down a few rocks in exchange for it. Then in room number three the guys deep-throat the other guy. The question of "whose better" them, or me and the show goes on. Anyway as our lives continued to slide downward, and the need to keep my children fed, clothed, and housed remained my greatest priority. But we did so. Even as we moved from place to place. In one place we moved to, we were given a block by a dealer each morning to work out of our house. Although that wasn't a lot if you considered he worked out of the house all day long. But of course, we did get more from him during the day. And he cried about that, but...

The situation was such that if a houseman, or housewoman smoked, they would be able to get hits during the day from people who score but needed someplace to smoke. So, they would ask you if they could hit in your place and then they would, of course, give you a hit or two for the privilege to hit in your house. Therefore, we were smoking throughout the day and night. But there were some dealers who played the game fairly. They would pay the rent and utilities. They would even give the house food sometimes. A lot of the smokers brought the food from the stores to the house in exchange for a hit or two. Then the house would get some of that from the dealers. This game had lots of twist and turns in it. In the end, all was well that ended well, that is, until the smokers hit slipped away. It would be surprising to a lot of people to know what went on inside some of these apartments and houses. The dealer took over the houses from people for a very small price. They would even bring in some of their workers from time to time to work out in somebody's house. They would take total control for a little or nothing. Again, the power of the rock.

Occasionally, the whore and johns would get down in the house. Sometimes the houseperson took care of it, and then other times the dealer would work it out with the house because the john would be a big spender. In cases like that, both the house and the dealers would profit from that kind of deal. For the houseperson, it was all about them getting the next hit. The smart houseperson would create their own hustle inside the house. They would twirl some of the product they got from either the dealer or customer. They would put their stem aside and go to work. If they were patient enough they could make some money. Although the dealer paid for the use of the house, they wouldn't beef because the money would come back to them, more times than not. We would set up an enterprise in our place and were able to make enough money or rocks that we would have some when everyone else had left.

However, before too long, the crack life separated me from my family. I went to my mom's house and my wife and children went to her mother's house, this was customary the way the program usually went. And…during those times when I was blasted from the cloudy mist of cocaine smoke, I had but one objective: to relive that euphoric feeling. My hands would continue their journey from the plate of rocks to stems, to lighter to stem to mouth. Each day I lived with the assumption that I had to have another and another hit! I had to zoom once again in that narcotic haze. To feel that blast which comes only when getting a *good hit* of that rock!

My cares and concerns beyond that rock were minimal. I gave little thought to where I would lay my head each night because I had no thought of lying down. I did not think about eating because, with the rock, there was no appetite for food. The only thing I wanted in my mouth was a stem filled with the chips of a "fifty" block of rock cocaine. Whenever that present rock was consumed and the high became a low, my "dopamine" brain compelled me to seek out methods, answers, and strategies, whatever to get back to that euphoric state of being. I would become a runner, or petty dealer for the dealer. This is when I would sell three or four for him, so I could get some to smoke. I would do just about anything to get that next hit. Hooked on that so-called good life, that high flying world of narcotics and glamorous interludes. I went about my business being all I could be while getting high. This was my life's cycle. My need/desire to have my mind blown was upmost in my life. I had gotten to the point where nothing else mattered in my life.

This, indeed, is a sad state to be in but it had become a way of life. It was my only life. I was hooked long before I knew it. Long before I realized it. That thing called "Scotty" had my body! Even though it was holding on to me, actually cutting off my life, I had no idea this was happening to me. When I thought my involvement with the rock was a temporary thing, my delusion was driving me further down the road to destruction and despair. When I was saying,

SPELLMAN BERNARD SMITH, JR. AKA SIR DOG

"I can handle it!" it was already out of hand and was handling me. When 1990 rolled in, I was rolling on the streets as a derelict! I had no place to call my home. I lived wherever I could, which usually was in or near, "The Hole." Which was the area where night or day, one of the biggest open-air drug markets flourished. When I did sleep, it usually was at the house of another "rock star." These people who smoked constantly, they usually banded together. We would sometimes hustle together, or we would go out separately, but would poll our resources to get something to smoke. These people had come from all walks of life, some of us had impeccable backgrounds, but we had one common bond, we were all hooked on rock cocaine. I've spent many nights or days, in old abandoned apartments, back stairwells, abandoned cars, wherever. I had couple of relatives who would occasionally let me crash at their place. One of them was a rock star also, so all I had to do was to have a small rock to gain entrance there.

At that time, I had only a few pieces of clothes. I think I had three pair pants, three shirts, and one pair of boots. When anything wore out, I would go to the store and to the walk-in exchange system to get what I needed. I stole my socks and underwear as needed. All this I carried with me in a gym bag. When I ate, I ate what I plucked off the shelves of the local grocery stores. Sometimes I would go into the large supermarkets, get me a carriage and go through the market like the other shoppers, but I would be eating all the while. I would stuff my shirt full of "quick selling items" and then leave. *I stole a lot of drug store items.* They sold well in the bootlegger's house as did meats, nylons, jewelry and such. Sometimes if a dealer gave me something to sell and he allowed me to get out of his sight for just a few moments, I would take off with the bag! I would deal with him whenever I saw him again. Sometimes I would hold a bag for someone if "5-0" rode into the area. That way I could earn at least a couple of twenties or a "fifty block."

I would be up two, three, even four days in succession. The days and nights sort of melted into each other and passed as blurs. Because if I wasn't smoking rock I was trying to get on. Sometimes I would take vacations from the scene. But, in retrospect, I think those were the times when I couldn't afford a hit because I was broke. Because as soon as I would get some money in my hands, I found myself being steered back to the hole. At a time when I thought that my participation in that drug scene was a temporary thing and would run its course and come to an honorable conclusion, I was living under a false illusion. My world as I had previously known it, was gone. I was gone. Yet I did not know it. The truth is, I was living in a zone far removed from the norm. I assumed that all was all right with me and when I got ready to, I would because I could bounce back to that ordinary drab and dull world of the "nondoers." I lived, yet, I was among the undead. I bordered on the edge of reality and illusionary. In essence, I had taken up residence in two worlds. I floated in and out of the world of reality when I was sober and the world of the undead when I was hooked on drugs. I had fallen to crack in the traditional way. Everything I did was to feed that constant desire to relive those euphoric moments. Every cent I got went toward the purchase of another rock. There were times when I wanted to get away from the drugs. I wanted to stop doing it. I wanted to stop smoking crack and get back to the real world.

Eventually, the wrong caught up with me. But before that happened, I had made an attempt feeble as it was an attempt, nonetheless, to rid myself of that dreadful addiction. In early January 1990, I checked into the Norfolk Community Service Board's substance abuse center. After being there for only a few days, I felt I was clear and that I had seen the light. I felt that I could now handle it. (How wrong I was.) I left the center with a new outlook on life. I was rested, well-fed, and ready, or so I thought to resume a normal life. Little did I know or remotely suspect that my troubles had not fully manifested themselves. I was in for a rude awakening. Before too long, I found myself back in the same old place, doing the same old thing. Along with everything else I did, I started cashing any kind and every kind of check I could. This started when I hooked up with a guy who did time with me in the penitentiary and the trailer camp. It was slick of me. All I had to do was to take the check to the bank, produce my ID, and they would give me the money, good!

My partner was different in a way that was strange to me. He was the only person I knew who had no desire for anything sexual when he took a hit. Initially, I thought he might be gay, but after he passed "my test," I concluded that he wasn't. He would go deep into his daddy's checkbook and get a couple of checks. He would make out a couple to me, and I would make out a couple to him. We would score heavy and smoke just as heavy. Some smokers would take a hit and savor its effect, while others hit with a consistence that lets you think they were in a hurry to get out of there. The only real problem with that is when two people are smoking out of the same plate together, the fast one will out smoke the slower smoker; thus, they'll get more. The best way to do that was as soon as you cook it up, you divide equally, then the only thing you have to be concerned about is the faster smoker asking you for some of yours. But you don't have to give them anything. Another thing was how we would fail to play fair. It's true that crack would bring out the worst of the worst out of us. Yet there were those who played fair with us.

This brings back memory the time when we hooked up with the brother who had a car. Which is a commodity of grand appreciation when none of us are driving. We went cigarette hustling one night. We chose a big supermarket that was close to us and was fair game. It displayed its cigarettes in a big display case and on the checkout lane. Plus, it opened twenty-four hours. All this made it a good picking. I could easily stack five or six cartons, forty to fifty packs. In fact, I once stashed fifty packs on me. All was good until I bent over to pick up my hard hat that I had dropped on the floor. I didn't know that the floor walker saw me, and when I headed out of the door there were two of them there to escort me back to the office.

However, when I went to court, I received favors from the judge. When I told her that I was a crack addict, and I stole these to support my habit she had me explain the process to her. I told her that we got five dollars a carton, or one dollar a pack, she nearly screamed. She thought that was so wrong. She sentenced me to a year's probation, suspended. A $100 fine was suspended. And banned me from the store for a year. In any, and all circumstances, cigarettes won hands down over everything else when it came to sell stolen items. The number one plus was the fact that we could sell them at any hour of the night or day. Another plus factor was the fact that we could sell them as packs as well as cartons. Most of the dealers smoked, and they preferred to make a deal with rocks rather than cash. Since that's what we wanted in the first place, that worked well for us. On this particular night, we were making a good score. Each of us had successfully made two trips to the car. My partner and I went out on our third trip back to the car only to find out that him and the car was gone. The dude had taken off! There's no telling how many cigarettes he had! This left us with about eighty to one hundred cigarettes on our person and no money or ride to make our get away. Also, the cigarettes we had on us were bulging all around us. Man! We were about two miles away from our spot and the alternative was to call a cab and run some kind of a game to him. He called a cab and gave him the address to the guy's girlfriend's house, and when we got there, he would have her pay the cabbie.

When we pulled up to the address my partner got out and went to knock on the door. In the meantime, I had the driver pull up to the corner and turn around and come back to the front of the building. When no one came out immediately, I got out grumbling and told the driver to wait a minute, and I went to the door. But I went past the door and went around the side and then knocked on the door that I knew my partner was in. I tapped on the door and went in to this broads place. We bagged up some cigarettes, and he carried them to a bootleggers' crib. When he came back, he had a pretty good-sized rock. I was okay with it but still wondered if he had stashed some rock for himself. He took a hit, I liked it, the broad liked it. And I liked her because she was a freak but since he wasn't, I had to wait until he left before I got into something freaky.

When he finally left, I exhaled a big sigh of relief. I had hid a piece of my share, and as soon as the door was closed and locked, the broad went into the bathroom to wash out that stuff. It was playtime. She sat down, took a hit, and did what she knew I want her to do. She spread those luscious thighs and flashed that big bush of hair. I took a hit and enjoyed the salute! I didn't hesitate any longer. On my knees I went and dropped my face into that big bush. I did what I enjoyed doing. To tell the truth, my little dick drippled some fluids and she gushed lots of fluid. At this point in my game, I'd gotten to the point where a broad, who was an expert in the finest of sucking a dick could raise the dead. Then I would pound that stuff like a pile driver for a total of two-and-half minutes. I was called the "two-and-a-half-minute man!" But both of us enjoyed me and her. Although my stroking was just two-and-a-half minutes that was enough for me. My masterful head was enough for her. You can't go wrong with that, and the beat goes on. A few days after, my partner and I went out looking for a score. He decided we could go to his woman's apartment to check it out. Anything we could trade in was good enough for us. When we got to her place, he had to go around the back of the building to get in and open the door for me. I sat down while he looked around the place. Eventually, he came across some checkbooks. Good! For me, this was better than finding some goods to exchange for money or rocks.

We got a cab and went to the bank. The checks were made out to me it was for some repair work I had done at her place. When we got to the bank, we parked beside a pawnshop that was across the street. I went in, and went right to the cashier. I presented her my ID along with the checks. She looked them over carefully and asked me to wait a minute. Then she went over to another desk to say something to another woman. They both looked at me. Well, I went out to tell my partner what was happening and to let him know that I didn't like how it looked. The cabdriver told me that he had gone into the pawnshop. I found him and told him what was happening. I went right back in and took my seat and began to read a magazine which is what I was doing when the police came in.

It was a fact that those checks came out of a book that was no longer active. The woman had another updated book. Therefore, I was busted from the get go. That's what the cashiers were discussing. I want to know what my partner was doing in the pawnshop. We supposedly didn't have anything else. Strange…

I was later tried and convicted of breaking and entering and attempted forgery. Wow, I was sentenced to four years. The sentence was weird because I couldn't understand how I got the breaking and entering charge. I told them I got into the apartment because he let me in to what I thought was his current girlfriend's house. Anyway

I was all right with four years. It was the shortest sentence I'd ever had. But while in the reception center of the hospital ward the police from Norfolk came to take me back to Norfolk. They didn't tell me what it was all about. But when I got there they took me to the Police Operation Center. They told me a bunch of crap, but the weirdest thing I've ever seen was the officer presented a photo face down and asked me to explain it.

Eventually, he told me it was a photo of me serving an undercover officer with twenty dollars piece of crack cocaine. But he still would not let me see the face of the photo. As I said, this was the strangest thing I'd ever seen or heard of. The thing is that I had served a bunch of people and could have easily served an officer, but when he told me where the transaction took place, I knew he was full of shit. They said I served the police at a location near the Lansdale Traffic Circle. If you know the dynamics of this scenario, you would know that no dealer would send a runner out that far for a twenty-dollar sale.

I work out of the "hole" which was at the Oakwood section not far from the Norview section of Norfolk. That spot was close to the airport and the old baseball diamond. Dumb. Real dumb! Yet in the end, I was sentenced to twenty years with ten suspended. Why? This meant that I ended up with a total of fourteen years. Why? People got that kind of time when they committed major crimes. The most confusing charges I've ever had. I went to Nottoway Correctional Center where I was reunited with some of my sons. Not real sons, but better and closer than blood sons. One of them was my number one son, Ervin Maddrey. We were as close as two guys could be. Our relationship went back to the days of the old state penitentiary in Richmond, Virginia. When I left him in Richmond, I went to improve my life and prepared a place for him to come home to.

It was while doing that time that I decided to write the first saga. Ervin was the person who helped me. He did all the typing, not just for Saga, but for most of it for the other nine booklets I wrote. There is history with my writings. While in the pen, I joined the United States Jaycees' and dedicated myself to it to the extent that I was elected president of our chapter the first year of my membership.

SPELLMAN BERNARD SMITH, JR. AKA SIR DOG

A historical milestone, no one had ever been elected president during their first year membership. Ervin, whom we called Popeye was or is a very smart man. One of the things we have in common is our level of knowledge and intelligence. His is such that he was able to get himself out of prison in twenty-one years. HE WAS SERVING LIFE PLUS SIXTY YEARS! I don't know any convict who was able to do that, and I've been serving time in prison since 1957! I love Popeye more than I love any other guy I know. Only my friend Bobby was as close to me, I had five sons. And we were tight as dicks hat band. We didn't have a gang, we were a family. Our ties were unbreakable. Those were the days before crack when we were weed smokers. Super bad smokers. And thanks to our female family members we were able to smoke daily. The most unique thing about my prison family was the ties that bonded us. Although my family wasn't a violent family, we could respond to such if it was necessary.

In my world of crack cocaine, the same principle holds true. I'm not a violent person, but if and when it became necessary I could do what needed to be done. There were a couple of times when a couple of stupid-ass dudes disrespected the woman who the whole world knew I loved. Although I didn't have to put my hands to them, I did let them know what could happen if they persisted. Actually, no one would dare challenge me. Especially since I had access to the shotgun (it was no good) and I constantly carried a butcher knife around with me all day long. I did seven-and-half year. I came home a reformed man. I had rededicated my life to Christ. I became a devoted Christian and tutor in our school. And I came home with an idea of serving people by providing transportation to prisons and to assist families of prisoners in various programs. My cousin gave me the money to pay for a van. Although the one I found didn't have seats, it was in good condition. And thanks be to God I found enough seats to fill it to capacity. I had a fifteen-passenger van. And once I got the seats, I knew I was ready to get down with my program.

When I got out, I was on probation. That was all right with me. I was living with my mom and my wife and children who were living with her mother. Although they lived in Portsmouth and I lived in Norfolk, we saw each other regularly. I would go get them on

Saturdays, and bring them over so we could go to church on Sunday. See, I was still active in my church and even carried my daughter with me to a church service with one of the churches that had visited us in the joint.

Everything was going along all right until I allowed my sexual propensity to get the best of me. Then I started tricking. I used to get crack to exchange for sex rather than using cash. I knew from experience that I got better programs from a trick if I presented rock instead of cash. I should have paid attention to my daughter who told me that if I was going to do a trick I should just give them the money. She said that I should not be putting that mess in my hands. How stupid can we be? Sometimes we think we know everything.

After I got my van we moved back down to Ocean View. We did our best to make things okay with our family. One of the things that happened to us was a windfall of epic proportion. It was the gift that was supposed to bring me and my family up, not carry us further down. At first I saw this as the gift from God. I believe that, as a child of God that he would provide all my needs, according to His riches in glory. See, I believe this, because despite how I act, what I do, or how I feel, I know that I am a true child of the true and living God. I know that this windfall was actually a blessing from the Most High God. How else can you explain what happened?

I got a letter from a loan company. The letter said if I want to borrow $5,000, check the box below. I did. Next I got a letter that said it was approved and that my check was on the way. Well, it came during that week. I carried it to my bank. The cashier said that it would take approximately three days, or so, to clear. She said that I should come back at the end of the week to check. I came back to check my account. It said that I had a deposit of $4,990 deposited to my account. Oh! What a deal. It was the best and worst thing that could happen to me in twenty years. What I thought was a blessing ended up being a curse. I abused the gift like you would never believe.

Yes, I did some good with the money. I filled the house up with grocery and household goods, bought the children some clothes and school supplies. I got my wife a nice used car, the one she wanted. And the last time I saw it a dealer was driving it off. The worst part about that is the fact that he made a partial payment and the product was what we call pure garbage. And yes, I did my thing, but mostly away from my wife. It got to the point that I did most of my smoking way from my wife because I always wanted to freak off, and she and I didn't do that much anymore.

However, there was a time when I wanted to freak off with this young gay boy. I had to pay her a sixteenth to let me have our place. Well, I paid her and she came back in no time at all. Of course, he and I hadn't done much of anything. And in order to finish the moment, I had to pay her more. That's the kind of games she played with me. There was a time when I was supposed to be introducing her to a broad so she could get it on. I wanted to see it and I wanted her to experience it. She said okay. Again I had to pay for it, of course. I went and got them a sixteenth. I brought it back and sit there and got one hit, then she asked me to give them a moment to get started, and then I could come back in. When I got back into the room, it was time to go get some more. I did. When I got back, I went for the same thing. In the end, I spent $400 and didn't see shit! That happened twice with two broads, both of them bisexual. I know that I was being used and I know they would do what I asked them to.

But with her, it was a different story. But I left her and went out on my own. I went where I knew I would find the real freaks. I went to the other gay guys' house. It was a hangout joint that catered to all of us who dealt in every sexual persuasion. After being there for a while, I called the house to see how my wife was doing. Of course, she asked me where I was. *None-u.* But some time later the guy told me that I had a call. Shocked the hell out of me when I realized that it was her. I had not given her the number and no one in the house knew how to reach her. That's when I found out about the method of calling a number back that called your number. There were about four bisexual women, a gay guy, and me. I was the one known as the all pro sex master. I was noted as being "trisexual," even though most people couldn't explain what a trisexual was. But we were doing what I love doing. Smoking and stroking. The girls were doing each other and I was trying to do something besides lick clits.

I made a deal for the whores. I put a thirty-cent piece on my navel and said whoever could raise the dead could have it. Hey! The girls all gave it their best shot. Now I was sure the gay boy could do it, but for some reason, he didn't want to do it in front of the girls. There was an all pro dick sucker in there who I also knew could do it. She could if anyone could. When the guys graded the best of the best, she always came up as number one. Oh! How I wish I could tell you her name! But I can't. But after watching all the other broads try, she said, "Step back, I'll show you whores how to suck a dick properly." She told me she'll take the rock now, and she did. And then she did what none of the others came close to doing. No one could come anywhere close to what she did. A pro is a pro. And that's what we were. I damn near rose up off the bed as she did something that was out of this world. She not only raised the dead, but she almost bought me to an explosive orgasm. But she stopped and told one of the other broads to lie back and let me pound into that stuff. I did… In fact, we did it on the floor of the closet.

We stayed there until the next morning, I then left with one of the fine asses. We went scored again. Smoke again, I got tired of her and went to the family house. I stashed my stack, took me a piece, and got me a change of clothes and went into the bathroom. Close and locked the door and took me a megahit and stepped into the shower. When I came out of there I ran into another dear friend who wanted to take me away from the house and carry me over to her cousin's house. I pulled my brother to the side and whispered in his ear. We then left the house with the freak and a bolder. We left a house full of people who were standing there with open mouths and sadness in their eyes.

The Life and Story of Spellman Bernard Smith

I never gave into desire to smoke. I would give them the product and they would do anything from a headstand to a "spread fandango." Then I met "her." She was absolutely exciting beyond expectation! The one thing different was that she told me that she would not do anything just for rocks. She told me that it was for money only. And if she wanted to she would buy my product, which is what she did. I paid for the work, and then she brought a bag from me. As she fired up, she asked me if I had to leave. I quickly replied, "No!" I sat and talked to her. As smart as I'm supposed to be, I should have smelled the rat. But no, I engaged her in casual conversation which was more of a "Q and A" session with her asking me about my past.

Yes, I used to smoke. No, I don't indulge anymore. She replied, "Why not?"

Because I don't like what it did to me. She brought another bag and told me she really like my product, and that she had a position for me. Outright she said she wanted me to smoke with her. Emphatically, no! She claimed she had a deal I could not refuse. Again, I tried to convince her that I no longer smoke I am not going that route. She said she would give me "some of this," she patted her pussy, and "some of this," she patted her mouth. She went as far as saying "And this" as she patted her butt!

I told her to pass me her stem as I reached for another bag. This all happened on a Friday night. We ended up parting company Monday afternoon. With her I found more ways to reach the mountaintop. In fact, we rode the celestial moonbeam to the Milky Way! She brought new meaning of reaching a climactically apex! She knew more of my sexual appetite than all the other girls before her. It mattered not what she did or what part of her body she used, she was able to bring me to more than two climaxes. It was so good being with her that it compelled me to go back to the house to get my stash of rocks and more money. This money I was saving to get a place for me and my family to move into. But this all pro sexologist compelled me to dig deep into my sexual manuals.

This encounter compelled me to reach to the top of the porno star's actions from the bygone era. When the deep-throat techniques and the expert use of the pole like instruments of deep vagina penetrations. Real deep! But her deep penetration was done with the longest tongue I've ever seen! One of the most amazing things of this encounter is the fact that not only was she capable of "raising the dead," but she kept it at attention for more than an hour.

This was the beginning of my engagement with that other addiction. What I call the "mighty relapse syndrome." See, I thought I would not do crack because I did not want to do crack. Oh! How true it is that addiction is cunning, baffling, and more powerful than a locomotive! It made me want to, and made me want to again, and again and again. It made feel as if I could leap tall buildings with a single hit! What I actually leaped into was a ride to the very north side of HELL! See, I could not continue to *not* smoke, simply because I *did not* want to smoke. I found that was one of those prevailing and quite personal myths. As I continue this, I will explain to you what I found about that part of the game known as "Relapsing." But just as I don't have all the answers about smoking, I certainly don't have all the answers about that part of the game, known as relapsing. Please, understand this, I mastered relapsing but failed the smoking game. But what I'm writing is what I found that typifies my life and times with what I call "mean relapse."

I want you to know that I thought I had mastered the concept of avoiding, or rejecting the major causes of my relapse problem which was what I needed to identify the major triggers in my drug life. Those things that I know would send me back on the road of using again. Such as; the people, the places, and the things. These warnings are ones I took seriously. I warned to avoid those things and people I knew would draw me into that particular lifestyle.

However, before really talking in depth about relapsing, I must first talk about my drug addiction. Although we might know what it is, does not mean we can adequately describe it. Question? What exactly is addiction? In the layman's term, addiction is the continuing extraordinarily strong desire, feeling, attachment, and/or yearning for something. For its seemingly irresistible attraction, it usually causes one to act compulsively and habitually stupid. And to indulge in activities usually of the negative nature. My level of addiction was beyond description. (I guess that's the real nature of addiction for everyone.) When asked how much crack I would smoke in a day, I could never give a precise answer. The amount of crack I smoked was determined only by the amount I could get. Unlike heroin users who usually have a prescribed amount of dope they would use at any time.

A crack smoker like me would smoke as long as it was available. And whenever the current supply was exhausted, I did what I could to get more. Its magnetism was incomparable! Its draw was stronger than anything else I knew. To be frank with you, I loved the way the drug made me feel even when I knew there would be agony coming thereafter. The high flying feeling surpassed any other feeling of pleasure I've ever experienced, which includes the sexual feeling! But trying to keep up with the feeling of that ride is more than I am able to do. There were times when I would become tired of the drug and the drug lifestyle. Perhaps, more of the lifestyle than the drug itself. Then, I became totally discombobulated, totally disgusted with myself my nasty, dirty self. And when I was sick and tired, or when I could see the forest for the trees, or when I did after a four-day run, fall back onto the washer. While trying to eat a sandwich, I would face the fact that it was time for a change in my life!

As I said before, there were times when I was down and looking up at the ceiling, all the while declaring, enough was enough! It was then that I would do something about it. First, I would check into the detox center. That was my five-day dry-out program. There I would receive my cleanup status.

From the center, I would go to the rehab facility, which was usually a twenty-eight-day treatment program. Early on my crack programming, I used my van as the method to get and do any, and everything. I became a fixture in my community with my van. My van stayed on the road, night and day. Some of the biggest hustlers in our community used me and my van on a daily basis. What kept me active was the fact that my van was a fifteen-passenger type. With all this room, it was unlimited what I could do inside it. I had two females, whom I called "Legs," who would spend days in the van were top-notch in what they do. They were noted for tricking. Most of what they tricked with was their educated heads.

We would roll up to the corner, and without a doubt, they have a customer in a matter of minutes. They used to brag about their skills when it came to giving head. When it came to giving head, they rated their skills from A to C. If they gave a guy an A head job it'll be over before we traveled a block down the street. I would hear the guy moan and sometimes let out a cry. She would then say, "Bernard, you can go back now."

I think they used to compete with each other to see who would *knock* the dude off the fastest. For me, the most important thing was they paid dimes, or rock, as they boarded the van as passenger do when they board the city bus. The girls shared theirs with me if they made a good score. But I wouldn't take theirs if I got a good hit from the john. Ferrying the girls around wasn't all I did. Some of the boosters the good thief rode that van on many missions. It was known that Bernard was available for a trip anytime, night or day.

I would take the dealers to do their pickup. There were times when I would be the official tester. Since dealers didn't smoke, they usually would choose someone when they considered to be equipped with a distinguished taste bud for crack as a tester. There was a dealer who used to run with me, but having done a bid was now doing his thing. He used to come by my house in the mornings and would bring me a hit to sample. I would call him later with my report.

Since one of the habits I had when I smoked was to slobber when I got a good hit; therefore, I would then tell him it was good by saying, slobber! when it was very good I would say double slob!

That's actually what I did! I had a lady friend who used to draped a bib around my neck and chest to catch the slob! When I tested for a dealer, I would then get a good deal of smoke. When that happened, there would be joy in the house. Then I would ask for a volunteer. Never failed to get one. They knew that they would get a double shot of pleasure: my head and a rock.

Ever since I first started getting my SSI monthly checks, I had celebrations. When I was not doing rocks, I would treat myself to a full meal and a movie, or two. However, once I started doing crack, I would rent a motel or hotel room. I would get drinks, weed, rocks, and a couple of volunteers. Of course, I would bring along my stick man. I made sure we got all the accessories that goes with the program: flames of some sort, chore boy, and extra stems. Each of these parties promised to be the party of the lifetime. Sex and drugs prevailed!

But the most baffling party I'd ever attended was presented by a woman who was giving herself a break out of an affair. She provided crack, weed, and alcohol. And lots of each. There was only two men and two women present. This promised to be the party of the year. She and I took our showers first, together. Went back into the bedroom, took a hit and drink, then played a little bit. Then the weirdest thing happened. The other said she had to leave! Why?

This was one of my "Legs," a lover of crack, and a person who never got enough. This baffled us. But when the other dude took his dick out, she mumbled that maybe she might stay. The brother had a python! But the show went on until something caused a rift in the setting. This caused me to walk out. Can't remember what it was all about, but I did enjoy the action until… Please, understand me, when I'm in the company of a person whom I loved personally and they flip the script like that it causes one to wonder or worry about her reason.

See, this particular woman life revolved around crack cocaine. Ordinarily, she would do just about anything for a hit. I've known her for a mere hit, suck a dick, and give up shot of body for seven dollars. So, when she stepped out from this party it gave cause to ponder. Then I came to the point where I could no longer deal with that miserable lifestyle. So I went to the detox center again. But unlike my first trip there, this time I saw that period through and went on to the rehab program. In five days, I was transferred to the green street program. It was my first time in one of those facilities and I found it to be quite informative. After being there for twenty-five days, I was dismissed from the program for inappropriate sexual activity with a female client. I was innocent of that charge. Therefore, I was dismissed.

When I left there, I was doing fine. I did not indulge in drug activities for months. I was attending Narcotics Anonymous (NA) meetings on a regular basis. My sponsor was a good man; I could call on him in times of need. However, in time, I did relapse. The irony of my relapse was precipitated by my association with a woman with whom I became friends with while attending NA meetings.

One of the things we were warned against was establishing intimate relationships with users. The reason for this proved itself to be prophetical. It is true that association brings on simulations.

In no time at all, I was back in the game. Though we started out together, this relationship didn't last very long, that, too, is a nature of the game. Very few relationships last for any length of time unless it's a couple who has been together for number of years. Anyway, let me say this, during the time I was clean and sober, my life was as good as one would hope it to be. And considering this, one would question why we would give up the *good* life for the troubling life of a user. Well, unless you've experienced the feeling one gets when hitting a stem of crack cocaine, you'll never know. And no one can adequately explain it to you. The one thing I can tell you is that desire to hit again burns within your dopamine brain.

No matter how hard you resist it, if you don't continue to fight that feeling, it will eventually overcome you. "Fight the good fight!" Of all the things I've done, none equals the role I played as a kidnapped guy. It was an academy award performance! I went to work at the club as I did nightly, and I carried some work with me. If the night went right, I could make a few bucks. However, it didn't go down that way. I ran into two of my old girlfriends. Instead of working, me and one of my old road dogs went with the women back to their crib. I had about three-fifty blocks and twenty-five-cent pieces. Although three seem like a lot of smoke, well, it isn't when you have four first class smokers who are smoking at will. We smoked throughout the night and morning. We ran the gambit of sexual proprieties, as well as we could.

When the last rock was consumed, I looked outside and wondered how was I going to explain to my wife, why I come home with no rocks or money. Ah! Ah! My ingenious streak burst upon my mind! First, I went to my car, and showed how it was ransacked by an intruder (me). Then I gave a guy money to make a phone call. I told him what to say and the time to make the call. I called my wife and told her I was kidnapped, and I just got out of the ropes, and that I'm trying to get home. I asked her to send me a cab. When I got home, I was shook-up. I told her how I was delivering some products to a guy's house, but after giving them a sample hit, the door was busted open, and two guys with guns drawn came into the room. They took all my money and my products. After putting a mask on my face, they carried me out. I had no deal where they carried me to, but once there they had me standing against a tree and they tied me to the tree with my arms hugging it. She gave me a hit, and while I was hitting it the phone rang. She screamed at the caller and asked them, "What did they do with my car?" When she hung up, she said the guy told her that the car was parked on a lot on Lafayette Boulevard. My daughter and her boyfriend took off to look for it. I took another hit.

My daughter came back about an hour later with my car. It wasn't damaged, although the interior was a bit disheveled.

Now, the most amazing thing about this is that it was the most exciting lie I'd ever manufactured. And it was three years later that I told her the truth. She questioned me one day when she came to visit me in prison. As I've said, there comes those times when I would become sick and tired of being sick and tired and then I would do something about it. Such a time came about in August of 1999. I checked into the detox center for my dry-out period. But I wanted more than just detoxing this time. But there weren't beds available any place. I was blessed to get an extension in the center. At the end of the second extension, someone gave me a number to call.

Although, it was an out of state number I called it, nonetheless. I was connected to a place called Dare County Drug and Alcohol Rehab center. It was in Kill Devil Hills, North Carolina.

The guy said something quite interesting. He said he would call me back to let me know *when* they would come to get me. And he did just that. I felt rescued! When he came to get me, the clerk attempted to give him some paperwork on me. He refused it. He said they're interested in the man and his soul.

There was another client who asked me to ask the man if he could take him also. Yes was the answer. In fact, they would take whoever wanted to go. One of the first things we were told when we got there was that isn't a ten anything program. It was a one person and that one was Jesus Christ. That program was operated by the Outer Branch Worship center. A church that preached Jesus Christ and him crucified. It was at this church that I rededicated my life to Christ. This program was longer than the previous rehab centers I'd been enrolled in. But my stay was one of the longest nonetheless. I went there in August. I was assigned to work in the thrift stores. We had three stores, and I eventually worked at all of them; I enjoyed it.

I enjoyed being in that program and enjoyed the church services. Having committed myself to the service of the Lord, I was loving it. The supervisor let me get a 1975 Lincoln Continental Mark IV. Super bad ride! I paid him eighty dollars down payment but the car was for my wife. Her current boyfriend brought her and the children to get the car and take me home for thanksgiving. Well, they came and we all went back to Virginia. We had a wonderful thanksgiving celebration. After a few days being with my family I went back to the program.

I had appeared to the superintendent to allow me to stay beyond the scheduled time. He had approved this and said I could stay as long as I needed to. I truly appreciated that. I was living a righteous life, dedicated to serving my Lord and Savior Jesus Christ.

After the Thanksgiving Day celebration, I drove our car back to house in North Carolina. I went back to work in the thrift store. The thing about that is, each place I worked at I was trusted with the daily receipts. This considering the fact that I was a user and ex-con.

After being back in the program I felt that I needed to get back home to my family and for my family. I told my supervisor as much. He agreed with me and help me prepare from my department.

One of the most touching thing that touched me was the generosity of another client in the program. First of all, he was giving me $400 to pay some court cost. But I asked him to make the checks out to my wife's landlord. I found out she was two months behind and was about to be evicted. He said no. He would give me checks to pay both my bills and my wife bills. This total was $1,600. We promised to send him the money back as soon as my wife was working and I was hustling. However, on my wife's first payday, she said she wasn't sending her the money anyplace. I paid the court my cost and cried.

Although we were living in Newport News, Virginia, I was still traveling to Norfolk to take pictures for parties, dances, and at the club. I was going to church regularly. Serving God was what I loved doing. I'd totally rededicated my life to Christ and prayed for the success of my family. My wife was doing well when I came back home. She worked at the Holiday Inn, and for a while, all was well. I wasn't doing drugs. Initially, my wife was living a clean and a sober life.

One payday, my wife did not come back home at all. She spent the night smoking up her check. When she finally came home, I asked her to get down on her knees with me and pray to God for forgiveness and strength to step away from the drugs. The following week she went to work and came home regularly. All was well for that week. However, on payday she failed to show up. I cried, just when I thought all was well, it wasn't. She didn't come home until the evening of the day after payday. When she came home, minus my phone and my camera. I was so mad that I felt like attacking her, but instead of doing something like that I chose to backslide.

I went downstairs and told the guy to go get me a fifty piece and bring *that* broad back with him. That was done in a matter of minutes. I was then living in a typical project like in most of our cities. This was the *hood*. It matter not what city I went to it wasn't hard to find the *hood*. Once it was there, no problem getting the two most requested commodities for a guy like me: rocks and hoes.

This particular broad was still carrying the body around that had not yet been devastated by rock. Not only did she have a fine ass, she also had legs. Love me some legs. Of course, she was willing to party with us. But after a while I was ready for a one-on-one program. But I was in this guy's house. What I did was to send him to get a sixteenth. When he came back, I asked him to step in the other room. I gave him a good six piece and told him, I wanted to be alone with the broad. No problem. So he came back into the room and got his stem and excused himself and went outside.

That procedure was customary in our world. People had no problem letting the big-time spender have their place. But if they didn't get an adequate piece of rock, it wouldn't be long before they'll be back knocking on the door. They would always want to wonder if they could get another *little* hit. That's why I tried to give them a sizable piece to start with. Anyway, when this woman took her clothes off, she displayed a most lusciously black body that one would expect to find on a much younger woman.

Of course, I introduced her to my salute game. Most of the time when this happened, she was butterball naked. She took a hit, lay back, and slowly began to rock those beautiful black thighs in and out, back and forward. I took my hit, and lo' and be'…Li'l Bernie began to rise! Now! This caught her off guard. Though the hit was as I like it to be the rise of my dick was shocking. I said, "Now!" This shock her…

Let me give you some history of this "Now!" command. When I'm lying and playing with a woman my dick is mostly in a relaxed position, the person would do those things that were designed to give rise to the occasion. One of the things women would do was to play with my nipples. My nipples are extremely sensitive and thoroughly enjoy manipulation. The nipple sucking, lip sucking, and my finger fucking her cunt could result in my dick rising.

When this is accomplished, I'd yell out, "Now!" She would then fall on her back, and I would mount her and push little Bernie into her cunt with the right stroke, it could get a full arousal. Then I would do my masterful stroking and most of the time it's beyond my normal two-and-half minutes. Anyway, like most of the encounters this was beyond my intensions of spending just a few dollars. And since I hadn't been doing anything, I had a few dollars in my pocket, thus a spending spree. I called the guy back into the room. I think I gave him $100 and asked him to get us something to drink and more rocks. After we consumed these, I left and went back upstairs to my apartment.

This was my first relapse period in quite a while. This was one of those relapse moment I attributed to my wife. Those of us who relapse usually attributed it to something or someone else. A part of the addiction world is blaming. Addicts have more reasons beyond themselves for their addiction. Most of the time it's the mate who causes us to relapse, or even for the first hit we took, and truth be told, a lot of time, it was other persuasions that initially tested us down that darken path. And it's true that my wife was the cause of me picking up again. But more times than not, it was some "Shamika" who was in the forefront of my march back on the battlefield of rock madness.

My battle with crack was not without blood, sweat, and lots of tears. Nor was it without my struggles to do the right thing. When I was in the Judeo Christian program things was looking very good. I can't remember how I got down there. My first step in recovery usually started with me checking into the Norfolk substance abuse center. This was the five-day cleanup program. Thus, I went to one of the twenty-eight-day program. Which was the Green Street Substance program in Portsmouth, Virginia. Like most program I think it's been shut down. Let me say this, I don't know why the powers be shut down the substance abuse program. If they thought these were going to be 100 percent success programs, and that's the reason they supported them, someone needed to have opened their eyes to the real world.

I believe the success of any of these programs was based upon the help that people got once they were discharged from those programs. If there was no help for them postrelease, their chances for success was slim to none! This also applies to ex-cons, to have a person serve out their sentence and then literally throw them back into society with nothing but an overly burden probation or parole officer to supervise them. Then, it's going to be tough for the *ex* to maintain their freedom. Sadly, this applies to an addict coming out of a rehab facility. I know I was one of those revolved door entities. Both rehab centers and correction facilities. Each time I came from either of them my desire, hopes and dreams were to become a successful citizen. Though I was smart enough to do so, I didn't.

Each time I relapsed it was a sneak attack. It came upon me in the dark of night and the brightness of day. It came upon me when I was with someone else, and it came upon me when I was alone. It came upon me when my mind was on the drug and it came upon me when the drug was far from my mind. It came upon me just a few hours after coming out of rehab, and it came upon me months, and years after coming out of rehab. For my relapses came upon me when it cared to. It seemed that the drug has a mind all its own. But it's ultimate goal was to render me helpless, soulless, weak, without constitution or the will to do what I really wanted to do.

Each time I relapse it was not a planned designed. In other words, I had not said to myself at any time of my enrollment in a program that when I was discharged that I was going to get me a hit. On the contrary, I would say just the opposite. I always thought I would utilize the skills and information I've gotten from the programs to survive in the streets. I excelled in every program I'd ever been in, whether I was incarcerated in the joints, or in the streets. More times than not, I was voted most likely to succeed. I became coordinator or assistant in most of those programs. However smart I think I am, or however, sharp others could perceive me to be, I've learned that crack cocaine can slay and burn me at any time I give it the opportunity to do so.

There were those times when I was quite certain I had won that battle. When I was able to say in voice, loud and clear. "I'm free or that mess!" I'm reminded of the first trip I took to Detroit. My daughter has said she wanted me to come up to be with the family. My wife had moved up there to get away from the world of crack cocaine. She had cleaned up and felt it would help to get away from the "people, places, and things," that played her in Virginia.

I sneaked away from my house and went over to stay with my oldest daughter for my last night in the Norfolk. I went to her house with my power stem. Brought me two twenties (I think) went in the room with the intention to fire up until the cab came to pick up me the next day for my trip to the bus station. However, after the first hit the urge for some sex overwhelmed me. Ah! Ha! At the apartment at the other end of the building was a homegirl from out or way. We had done it before and we both loved it. She was masterful with her head and loved my head to the hilt! Besides, we stroked good together. I went down and invited her to slid down to the crib for some good smoke and good loving.

We balled until daybreak. We had it made because she brought rocks with her. This what set her apart from most broads. From our first encounter, we hit off perfectly. So far, those last few hours in Norfolk I had a ball. When I boarded the bus, I was all right after few hours into the ride I actually fell asleep. When we rode into Washington, DC, I went into the bathroom to push my demo. The joint was loaded! It was a good hit. In fact, the second push was super! I then walked outside for some air. We had a two-hour layover. As soon as I hit the sidewalk, I saw "Him." I had never met him, but smoker was all over him. I went over to him and without introduction, or question I told him that I wanted him to get us a dub (twenty dollars). I was adamant. I said, "Look, I don't want no shit. I'm not going into the ally to score, but I expect you to get this and come right back."

He said, "Of course, yeah!" I know the mentality of a smoker. Although my approach was unorthodox he was glad to have met me. The boy needed a hit. We walked across the street to the entrance to an alleyway.

We stopped, I gave him the money. When he told me to wait right there, a voice from the dark ally said, "What's up?" I damn near shitted on myself. The dude told the voice that we had come to get a dub.

Let me hit you to something. I had a cousin who was a masterful hustler. He had a weed business at home. He would come to score weed from people up there through his brother who lived in DC. He did his business on a straight business level. Just him and his road dog would make the triple. He goes directly to his brothers, pick up the package, then turn around and come straight back home.

On one particular day, he did things out of character he carried two burr headed bitches with him. First thing out of character. When he got to his brother's place the packages hadn't arrived. He became impatient and was out looking for some himself. Out of character. He went on some street in Northwest DC in search. He met a stripper who told him, yes, he could get him whatever he wanted. His road dog was at his side doing this time.

However, when he went with the guy to score he went by himself. Out of character again. His road dog reported they crossed the street and went into an ally. Out of character. Next thing was shots being fired. When the road dog went to the alley my cousin was stretched out on the ground with blood coming out of his chest.

Thus, I declared I'd never go into an ally with someone for a transaction. Anyway, the dude came right back and put a decent size rock in my hand and said come on. He said we wouldn't have to go far and we didn't. It was an apartment building. There were seats around the sidewalk that was *L* shaped. People were sitting out like it was in the park. And there were constant flicking and no talk, or little talk. He and I went and sat down on some steps leading downward. The stuff was *good*. The one thing that bothered me was with the hit, the urge to do something! But I didn't. I suppressed the desire and flew high into the right sky.

After being there for a while, I checked my watch because I couldn't let the bus leave me. Good time! Actually time for more, if…I told him that I had enough time for more if he could and would go back to get another one and bring it back and not shit me. He promised me he would and offered to leave his jacket as collateral. I trusted him. When he left, Shanika came sliding up, asking could she join the party. I told her something about we not having much. She offered a shot of head for a hit. Anyway, dude came back in a hurry. He sent her packing. He said to her about how they didn't give him a hit when they ware smoking. Huh? Damn, it was my stuff. Anyway in a few minutes, I broke off a piece and told him to put it in his pocket. We smoked the rest and I jetted to the bus station. I got there a few moments before departure time and went into the restroom and into a stall. Sit on the stool and fired up my last hits then threw my stem into the trash can. In about eight minutes, I was on my way to Detroit, Michigan, for the first time in my life.

This was October of 2005. The one thing I experienced in that city was the fact that, I had no desire to smoke any crack. But not only was that experienced that time, but at no time. When I went to Detroit did I have a desire to smoke. However, every time I came back to Norfolk, I found myself back in the mix. I never understood what was the motivation factor. I know for sure it wasn't the people, because the time when I would ask someone to score for me they would initially refuse to do so.

I came back home in January of 2006, because I had found out my mom was seriously ill. She got tired and left us after I go back home not long after she passed away. The house became known as "The Trap." My brother and I went off the chain. Our house was the house to visit if you wanted to have a good time. This was my second house. I started out renting an apartment from my mom. One of those times where I came home from prison. For a million dollars, I couldn't tell you what I'd gotten locked up for. But I moved into Momma's apartment. I was doing extremely fine. In fact, I did fifteen months clean and sober. My anniversary celebration was held at the Social Service building. My home girl who was doing good work in her sobriety spoke at my celebration, it was an unbelievable good time in my life.

This was fifteen months of peace and joy. It lasted until the day one of my "legs" girlfriends came over to turn a trick. They gave me a couple of shots of gin in addition to twenty dollars. By the time they finished doing their do, I was tipsy. My brother came over and he went to score a fifty piece for "legs." She was back in the kitchen and I was up front doing work on my word machine. I took a break to go back to the bathroom. When I opened the door, she was hitting on the stem. I saw the smoker going through the stem and instantly the craving for a hit, it hit me like a bolt of lightning. I told her to give me that demo (the other name for a stem) she refused. She said,

"No!" Uncle Bernie, I'm not giving you this stuff." I told her to give me the demo, and a hit and the lighter. I took that hit. Which was the first step back on the road to destruction, and then it was on like a stone.

My apartment got to be called "The Bernard's place" or "The Yellow house." It consisted of a front room, middle room, kitchen, bathroom and a closet in a small front porch. Initially, the middle room was my bedroom and the front room, and the kitchen was the smoking room. Oh! The bathroom was also used as a utility room. There were orgies performed in there. I'll never forget the night my brother was out back by the window and called to ask who was in the bathroom.

I said, "I'm in here."

And another deep voice said, "Me too."

Bernard's place was continuing its legacy from the days of yesteryear. Only this time, it was rock cocaine rather than the original product weed. This house was the finest crack facility in the region, not because of its furnishing, but because of its attitude and disposition. Its versatility was immeasurable. It's always been my aim to please. I was always willing to assist my guest in their quest to achieve fulfillment in their pursuit of choice. I was the on-site dealer, or I would be the runner. When there wasn't anything on-site people had no hesitation to put their money in my hands to go score for them.

This is something you can't do with just anybody. Putting money into hands of a crack addict to score for you is chancy to say the least. My house had, or mostly had permanent residents. Among them was my favorite friend. This person shared my bed exclusively, and her place has the rights of a queen throne. The most satisfying aspect of this arrangement was whoever she was with, it was an acceptable fact that I had the right to my two-and-half minutes whenever I wanted them.

Attention, as I said previously this story is not laid out in chronological order, but is revealed as I recalled it. Each of the females who came to my place were generally available to me. What made this so exceptional is that it mattered not if they had a man. The reason why I might not do it to them, or the other, I just didn't want to do it to them. The dealers use to drop me packages to work. First of all, it was an advantage for them because smokers came at any time of the night or day. And dealers would sometime miss a sale because they couldn't make it in time.

They usually would drop me off a package with thirteen or fourteen dimes in it. That would be ten for them and the rest for me. Which was a workable deal. But I tightened up my side by opening up all the dimes and chopping off the "heads." I could easily do this because the rocks I got from the guys were good-sized. Then I would pack them up again and go to work. I always ended up with enough for a party. I used to always say, "Can I get a volunteer?" The answer was always, "Yes!" Most of the time, it would be me and one of my brothers, my favorite brothers. When he wasn't there I would indulge in various degrees of sexual exploration.

There was a time when a woman had quality looks and size was visiting the hot room with me and my brothers. She was sitting across from me. Wow! Not knowing it, she was presenting salute action to me without hesitation. I asked her would she like a shot of head. She said no, because she didn't like it. We interrogated her relentlessly. She finally said yes. I position her on the mat. She took off her pants and panties. What an elegant mount of venues! We both took another hit and she lay back and spread those luscious thighs, ass propped up on a pillow up to her knees. Slowly, I lowered my head down between those tan thighs. I approached that fat cunt with caution. I slowly traveled the length of the labia with this instrument of sheer erotic pleasure.

I turned my head on autopilot and my tongue on cruise control and sent her to a higher orgasmic pleasure where she'd never knew existed. The movement of hips buttocks and legs told my brother and I that she was in foreign territory of sexual pleasure. As her heaving belly trembled and the hissing, guttery sounds were emitting from her clenched teeth. I knew this was needed for her and possibly there would soon be a gushing climate eruption of fluids never been experienced by her.

As I thought on it, it came! She screamed and fluids covered my face. Her body trembled and she pushed my head up, and looked into my face with a look of sheer terror. The poor woman uttered words like those from the mother land. I moved away, put some cover over her, and gave her time to recover. Ah! Again, I had awakened a deep and unknown dream, which was residing unknowingly in this fine woman. She dropped off to sleep. My brother and I loaded up our demons and took another good hit and watched over her until she woke up. All this really wasn't new to us. When she did awaken, and got herself together we passed the peace pipes around again and laughed about the episode.

Readily she started to explain what she felt like. She testified that was unlike anything she ever experienced. And admitted that it was the best nut she'd ever had. More so than not she doesn't know what to say. My life was wrapped around crack and all it meant. I committed myself to the program of getting high on crack cocaine. Through one of my gay friends, I met up with this guy who ran a check cashing scheme. What he did was to write checks out to us coming from some fictitious company or organization and the checks were written for $900 or more. They were divided in three parts; me, the guy who brought them to me, and the writer.

They were designed so each party would get at least $300 each. I had no fear or problem in passing these. That is until I got busted. I really don't remember the specific details of how I got busted. Considering this thought, it's amazing how I can recall incidents so vividly. While others I had trouble putting everything together but one thing for certain, I'm not going to lie to add drama or glitz to this saga. I'm going to tell you the truth and nothing but the truth so help me.

With that said, let me continue with this *Saga of a Crack Addict*, know for sure that this saga is filled with episodes after episodes describing what that crack world is or was all about.

I remember when I got that first bust for checks, I also got an additional charge of distribution. The irony of that is that I was innocent of that charge, yet I got more time than I did for all the real shit I did, with the exception of the back shot. However, let me tell you of my life and times of renting from my mom in "Yellow house." As I was saying my mom was renting the apartment out to me and

I had the longest amount of clean time while I was there. During the first fifteen months when I was clean, I spent many nights at an NA meeting. I enjoyed going to meetings and fellowship with fellow members who were dedicated to the clean life.

As we say NA won't clean you up, but for me fellowshipping helped me stay clean. When one would share, it was inspirational, for one thing their sharing inspired me to continue on and keeping on. Although it was sad to hear when someone crashed, it was encouraging to hear others tell them the message of recovery. I learned that one could never fall so low that they can't get back up. As always, I was in control of things because there were so many dealers who like my hustle; I, for the most part, kept rocks. The worst part about this game of mind was my playtime.

As a smoker, I dedicated more time and effort to playing than I did working. Yeah, I worked my ass off making the dealers rich, but I played with my share. Yes, there were those times when their shares came up short. But that was expected, but the fact of the matter that I could turn *well*. There were times when their share was supposed to be $100, but they would get $70 or so. Sometimes they would take out their share from the next batch. So I ordinally would I get a package of ten dimes and three, but if I was short of $30 to then they would just give me ten, which meant I would be working off my debt.

But the fact of the matter was, they learned quickly that didn't work. Sometimes, I would work that out with them but, the fact of the matter is since I "took the heads" off them anyway I still came out all right. I wouldn't take small rocks from them. It was a fact that I'm so good at the game that I could easily insist that they kicked up the game or I wouldn't deal with it. There were times when I would dip with the package. If I ran into an alley, I could easily get lost.

There was a couple of times when I had just scored a package and the police showed up just as the dealer was leaving. I would escape them one way or the other. I would contact the dealer an hour so later to let him know I had to dash the product. They believed me because they would know somehow that the man would come to my house.

There was an incident when I had gotten my package off the head before I went to work. A broad came back to get over on me by telling the dude that the bags they'd gotten from me were *real* small. Well, he straightens that out by telling them he had nothing to do with that because what I did with those bags was my business and he didn't care. As long as I gave him his money. One could never imagine what goes in the crib like ours. But unlike most house, my house had a sense of hospitality for my guest, our rules were simple and few.

Simply put, one could not beg anyone else for a hit. It mattered not what you might have brought with you, or bought, or whom you might have given some to. No man could touch any women in the house. If a guy spent hundreds of dollars on a woman and had struck up a deal with her, he couldn't press her for anything.

If a dude wanted to trick with a broad and she agreed. He rented the room from me for ten to twenty dollars plus a hit. Okay. If the broad went into zipville, that's it until she come back. The guy just has to wait. I had a fine six-feet-tall white girl that was literally given to me. She was dedicated to Uncle Bernie and Uncle Bernie was dedicated to her. When she took a hit she would stand up in a boxer's stare. There she would be for a while. Nothing moved on her. Now, I would tell the tricks *do not give her hit until after!*"

More times than not they would chose to give her hit, and then would come get me. Before we would get in the door, I'd ask them had they given her a hit and stupid-like ignorance though they'll say, "Yes." Well, I would tell them "You just got to wait." No! They had to give her a hit because they thought that would make her quicker and better. When that didn't happen, they wanted some of their money back from both her and me. And if they persisted they would get escorted to the door. One thing I'm thankful for is that despite all the different kind of sex partners I had, I never got a case of any kind of venereal diseases! Some contracted VD and HIV, but we, my brother, and I were blessed.

There's no way I could tell you how many different women I've had. I can't tell you how many men I've had. And though I can say what I've done, I dare not tell you with whom I did it. After all, this is the *Saga of A Crack Addict*, my story only. However, I'm sure there will be lots of people looking for this book once it hits the shelf. Some out of curiosity, while some out of fear. But I've assured them I wouldn't reveal their IDs. Actually, it'll serve no useful purpose. But one things for sure, if I wasn't writing this story I would be interested in reading it!

There were some funny episodes happening in those three rooms, on to the funnies involved in the "real rock" episode. It was one of those slow days and nobody was around but my brother Charles and I. Like so many times we had a little bit of rock and was trying to hold it until one of the "burn heads" came home. But soon as we did it in, here, she comes. At that time, he went back to the house for something. Now, the broad was really family. Lo and behold, there was a real dirt rock in the dish on the dresser!

She became as excited as a cold miner who spied the mother lode. She went to touch it, but I told her I couldn't split it until Charles got back because it wasn't mine.

We sat there for a while with her trying to convince me to chip a hit off it. I kept saying no! Finally, I told her that I would go over and ask him could we get a hit off it. When I came back I told her he said wait. But then I told her to let me get a shot of that stuff and whether he was back, or not I was going to take a hit for her and I.

Well, the draws came off in record time. And as you know by now, the two-and-a-half minute guy did his thing. I told her to go clean that stuff out and when she got back, I'll give her a shot of head. As she took a hit of course she said yes. She took a quickie and came rushing back. I told her to take the blade and chip her off a good hit. Ha! She took that razor blade and put it to the rock, and mother… She said something about being hard as shit. Oh! I did the best I could to hold back the laughter. I acted like I'd become impatient and told her to give me the blade. As I was getting off the bed, Charles came in right away. She was telling him how hard the rock was.

Oh! he exclaimed. "Bernard, is that what you're talking about man! That isn't real. Besides, I think we hit the last piece before I went to the house." Oh, well! Another time in the life of the two brothers. We were closer than my other two brothers, I guess that's because Charles and I were a lot closer in age, but that's not exactly the real reason. I was much closer in age than 95 percent of the people I dealt with. There was a night, I think it was the night when we decided to play switch with the two women we were dealing with. One of them was his current part-time piece, while the other one was a visitor, but she was with me.

Let me explain my brother and I. We operated the "Chuck and Bernie show." We were noted for our particular sexual expertise. Some of the broad called him "Diamond Dick." While some said he had a magic dick. There was one broad who said he had a "demon dick." In fact, this burr headed broad had me set them up for her first encounter with that dick. She had a package to get that dick. I even had to babysit Charles's other woman while he pounded the shit out of this curious bitch. They rocked and rolled and smoked for hours. The thing about this is that they didn't share one rock with me. And in the end I took the fall for the loss of her package to her old man. This wasn't the only time I bailed her out. We were tight, or so we supposed to have been. But other shit came eventually about that certified saying, "Keep your friend close and your enemies closer." Check this episode out!

Anyway, as I was saying the Chuck and Bernie show was enjoyed by a number of women. He had the masterful dick and I had the head extraordinaire! On this one particular night, we had decided we were going to switch up. Not that the women know or that they had to give their consent. When the time came to do it, we simultaneously told them that they were to go into the other room with the other brother. Although this was a surprise to them, there was no objecting. Both of us had already knocked off one of them, but the other broad was experiencing us for the first time. She got some of this golden head. Something she'd never experienced in her lifetime. And she was blown away like the women who are getting this head for the first time. When both couples finished round one, separately, we all came together in my room to engage in common smoking. We laughed and smoked a couple of rocks, and then we took the other broad in our respective rooms. It didn't take a lot of persuasion to do it. And no one was disappointed in what we got from the other particular part. This was one of the times when there was no open door. We were home all alone!

Also, this is the kind of activity that drove little Bernard beyond the a two-and-half minute episodes. And because it was a longer time, I would get a harder, longer tool to work with. Also, I too, could stroke very well. Sex was a family trademark. In fact, before there was crack for us, we did weed at that time the Chuck and Bernie show existed. And there were scores of women who were blessed by these brothers. That brings to mind the big girl we met from Virginia Beach. She explained to us of how her man rejected her. She had to literally beg him for sex. How the dog didn't respond playfully with her anymore. In fact, nothing positive happen in her life. Well, we got her to come with us to the "little house." That was a two-room cabin in our backyard. It started out as a one room cabin in 1955. That became my room when I came home from the Air Force in 1956, and my first daughter was conceived out there.

Anyway, this was 1983 when Charles and I carried her out there. The only thing missing of that was the filming of all the women we've share our stuff with. Her orgasms were countless. Her tears flowed by the quarts.

When we carried her back home early that next morning, she was the happiest, most complete women I'd ever seen. Her gratitude was expressed every day for the rest of the month. She called our house every day. Momma wanted to know what did we do to her to cause her to call every day. When we talked with her she said since that night her whole life changed. Her husband treated her much better. The dog wanted to play with her all the time. The flowers started to bloom! Not lying. Speaking of the little house, first of all, it was notorious for its constant activities. Its history covered about thirty-five years and a couple of innovations done to it. Uncle Tom converted my original room to a kitchen and added a bathroom between the two cabins.

In its later years, it was reduced to one cabin which could accommodate an untold number of rock stars, or crackheads for nightly smoke out. We used that shed until the day I dropped it. Let me explain first of all how that little place served the needs of the crack community, relentlessly, night and day. There were representatives from every race, nation, persuasion, and genders. The United Nation could have used the concept of the brotherhood of how mankind know could coexist with another. There was such degree of camaraderie that you could walk up to a broad and get a shot of head while you hit your demo. It happens to be in there when someone came in with a rock and no hitter. You were assured of getting one if you had a stem, and more so if your stem was glass.

The little house did not have heat in the winter, or air condition on the summer, but we survived. The primary concern was that this was a place where one could come and smoke. Our community had the pleasure of having police officers who were passionate and actually loved, and respected my mother. They would protect her to the extent that when her last son was on the street and was wanted, or has committed a minor offense that they would stay around and not abandon their mother. I've seen one come out and examine my little house and discover paraphernalia and merely order Charles to clean the place up. See, it was widely known that it was Charles's little house. It's hard to adequately describe the little house. But one of the biggest mistakes I've ever made in my life was to tear it down. I did so because I misunderstood what my mother meant when she said she was tired of that constant traffic coming through the yard.

She told me this one day when we were sitting in the backyard, which was the divide between the house and the little house. For the most part no one comes through there if she was sitting out here. Every once in a while, someone would come through there who was a longtime family friend. They would speak and ask if could the come through the yard. I remember one summer day there was a few of us were in there. Then Mom came outside with her soda and took her seat in shade. There were those of us sweating like slaves in the master's fields! Everyone was afraid to go out because they didn't want to be seen by her. Not that she would have done anything, but out of respect of the rules that moment. The funny part about this is that she knew we were trapped in that hot-ass place! Eventually, one of our family lifetime friends said, enough and she open door, step out through the door followed by a wave of steam and smoke.

She said, "Hello, Mom…" Mom smiled and said hello.

She said something like, "I know you're hot, ain't you?" And that was the signature and everyone poured out of there like refugees falling out of the hole of a transport. Anyway, when she told me she was tired of the foot traffic, I took that to mean that she wanted it out of the way. So, I took it down. I never got so many enemies at any one time, over one thing as I did then. Even when I went to jail there were guys who asked if it was true that I tore down the little house. I thought I was going to be attack!

When I went to prison these were the guys who questioned me about tearing down the little house. You would think I torn down some sort of shrine. Well, in a way it was. To add injury to insult, Mom told my ex-wife that I tore it down because they wouldn't let me in to smoke with them (smile)! At times, the little house was used when other facilities we had were filled to capacity, or when someone wanted to isolate them and the other from others. When I refer to the yellow house, I'm talking about a side of the duplex my mom owned and rented out. When I first moved in the yellow house it was a rental property. I was doing all right. It was in there that I sold a record of clean living when I had celebrated my one-year anniversary. I did fifteen clean months while living there. The weirdest thing about my experience in that place was that my sister *allowed* a friend of hers to live there, free of charge, while I was required to pay my mom rent. But it eventually turned out to be good for me. The guy turned out to being a very good friend to me. We shared many wonderful moments together. We shared the pleasure of a pleasant young gay guy. At one point, I thought the gay guy was on the verge of getting married. He was a good guy. Very generous and good at everything he did. We spent many hours smoking bags of crack. He had no problem spending his money. He had a friend whom he could trust with his card to get his money. Throughout the night, he would send him to the machine and he would bring all the money back.

One night, while he was on a run, I asked the gay was that dude getting that stuff. I was surprised when he said no, but that he wanted that dick. Well, when he came back, I brought the conversation up and asked him why he hadn't given the *boy* the dick. I can't remember exactly what the answer was but, he did give it to him that night. And what a dick it was! It started with the boy kneeling on the bed from the side. The dude stood up beside the bed and entered into that good ass with the kind pole most white people attribute black guys with having! They said it was the first time, but it's hard for me to believe that. The boy had his cute little black ass hunched up and this guy was stroking it like they'd been at it for years! This was one of those times when I'd sit back in my chair and beat my dick. It was just that exciting! The gay guy got to be very good friends. In fact, it was he who introduced me to the guy with the checks. There were a number of us who eventually got busted for the checks. All this originated in Bernard's place, the yellow house.

The Sage of a Crack Addict is a long, long story that involved number of people from all points of the globe. We dedicated our lives to getting another hit of rock cocaine. We had no qualms about what we had to do to get that next right hit. It mattered not that we had to hunt, rob, trick, or trade, to get that next hit. Understand it's more about the *next* hit. See, getting that first hit was usually based upon when, not how. We usually had money or was with someone who had money and they carried you along with them the first time around. When we had money or an acquaintance had money it was mostly a matter of getting a hit. Then when that money was exhausted it becomes a job to get those next hits. Those and the "boo-boo" hits. Which are the hit you cried for. At some point, I again was locked up. When I came home it wasn't long before my daughter decided that I should go up to Detroit. It was a surprise trip. As far as my wife was concerned. It was really a surprise to my wife. But it wasn't a pleasant surprise. I think I was the last person she wanted to see. It became apparent just how much she didn't want to see me. It was when she refused to sleep in the bed with me and she wouldn't even give me a shot of stuff. Although we weren't together, I was still her husband, and as such I thought I was entitled to some of that stuff. And the truth of the matter is that I loved that fat juicy stuff! I got some on check day! She didn't want it to seem like a trick, but that's what it was. Initially, I was satisfied with that. But when she attempted to fake an orgasm, well, that was too much.

Amazingly, I had no desire to smoke a rock. I wanted nothing. I found me a good Bible, filled the church up around the corner. I met those people as I walked around looking for food for thanksgiving. At first, their reply was like the other churches that said I was too late. As I was leaving one of the brothers stopped me. They said wait a minute they were sure they could find me something. They not only found me something, but a young man carried me home with my food. We greatly appreciated that. From that day on, I became a dedicated member to that church. I loved their fellowship. It was as if I'd been a member of that congregation for years. Brother Keith and I became the very best of friends as was our families. One of the most amazing things happened to me is the fact that I lost all desire to do drugs. Not only crack but any other drug or drink. This was a phenomenal effect that this city had on me. All was well with me while I was in the city of Detroit. I tricked only twice in all the time I'd been there, and smoked some weed a couple of times. Other than that, I've been clean and sober. My first stay there was cut short when I called home to wish everyone a Merry Christmas. It was then that I learned my mother was back in the hospital. Problem begins is when I was never told that she had been there in the first place. Not had she been home, but she had been in the intensive care unit. And even at this time she was doing poorly.

My problem was that I was broke and I couldn't get back to Norfolk. No one was willing or able to help me. I had to wait until I got my monthly SSI check. Well, I got home as soon as I could, which was about the third of January 2006. Mom had gotten home from the hospital by that time and she was still sick. Charles was home and he took care of Mommy in a very fine way. He cooked for her and did everything needed to be done with for her except bathing. Our cousin Margaret did that.

Margaret was the one who administered to Mom in a way more so than any other person than Charles. When it was time for Mom to go to her dialysis treatment that was my assignment. Three times a week, I accompanied her to treatment. I wouldn't have it any other way.

Later on when Mom was confined to the hospital, that was my daily assignment. There was a slight misunderstanding between the staff and me. At the end of visiting hours the nurses told me that I'd had to leave. I politely told her that I couldn't leave until my mom said it was all right to do so. See the so-called end of visiting hours wasn't meant to apply to Mom's sons. I can't forget how it was that my time was Mom's time. I moved in with my daughter because she lived within walking distance to Mom.

Mom, passed away on my daughter's birthday. Then my oldest daughter passed away on the same date eight years later, which is four days after mine and my other daughter's birthday. (Coincidental, as I'm now writing this, I just met a nice woman whose birthday is the twenty-eighth.) My mom came home to live out her final days. She was under hospice care for days. Although she was unconscious she remained with us until her niece came home from Nebraska. We felt that Mom stayed here long enough for my niece to be home to say goodbye to her grandmother. Little did we know it, but our house was to become known as "the trap." Because if you come to this house you became trapped. Once there nobody wanted to leave. Charles had the back bedroom, which became to be known as apartment A. My room became known as apartment B. Although each was reknown crack spot, each had its own idiosyncrasy personality.

There were those times when some people, mostly women, would start out in apartment B but would slide down to Charles's room. The motivated reason for the women moving down to apartment A is for the possibility of getting a shot of that Mandingo dick! There were times when they would come with the hopes of double dialing. They either had some product or the money to score with. They knew we could flip the product. Therefore, they could smoke and twirl.

I would help them with the understanding that they would have to be patient. Although we could deal the produce, there were times when there was a lure in the time when the buyers would show up. Considering this, I would tell them that they would have to smoke wisely. If they smoked up their product, too bad! They would have no more. And what did they do? Smoked up their shit in Charles's room and was then put out. And came back crying to me. See, he would put them out when they became broke and I'd have to hear them boo hooing! Most of the nights, I would have four or more females in my room. Sometimes they would have something of their own and we would share it and the pussy with me. This is the everlasting program of Bernard and his bag of hoes. Although they weren't technically mine, they were mine nonetheless. I could share more stories with you, but they're repetitive. We did the same thing over, and over again. I fucked and sucked an untold number of slutty-ass hoes.

My dick was sucked by both men and women. I've always prefer head from men for the most part. What make men better at sucking dicks is the same concept that make women better than men when it comes to sucking pussy. I feel that the approach is manifested by the fact that since you possess the like organ your approach is based on the fact we know the area and motions that excites us. Therefore, when a woman lick a cunt they do it as they like done to them; same with a man. Then there are people like me who have created games and other approach to doing it to either of the sexes is based on the fact that, I have a sense of creativity that most people don't possess. The reason I was a top-notch trisexual is because I search out ways that bring either of them to an orgasm with atomic-bomb-like explosion.

Mom was a loving, caring mother to her five children, four stupid-ass boys and one girl. Early on three of her boys went to prison, which her oldest, me going in the earliest with the bigger sentence.

Charles stayed home. When crack became a thing of choice, my brothers became victims early on. They would get in trouble with the dealers and at times would pay the price for violating the rules of the game, one way or the other. Out of concern for the safety of her sons, Mom allowed it. First Charles, then all of us to hit in the back room. When she moved into the dining room Charles moved into her room. That room became the den of in ingenuity. The front window was the entrance point. This allowed people to come in so Mom wouldn't see them. But Mom had that keen perception that told her when she came through the window. Mom would call Charles to tell that girl to leave. It was after she passed away that it became my room.

It was a delight. A sanctuary for the lonely, down trotter and anything else you could think of. If some were to come with a bag, of course they were welcomed. If you had some money you could usually find someone who could accommodate you As. I sit here writing from my memory, my mind is being inundated with countless images from that by gone era. If I were to tell you this incident that happened that day and time, I'll see several others identical to that one. But there was a moment that I'll stand out into all eternity. That was the day I realized I was in love with her. See, I'd been a fan of hers for a long time. Even when I was in the company with her and either of her boyfriends, I had this feeling for her.

But on this one particular morning, she had awakened me as usual, and like this time, she had something for me. She literally fed me a hit. Unlike any other time of our encounters something happened when I took my hit, I looked up into her beautiful face. But unlike any other time, I was overwhelmed by a rushed feeling that transformed her into a princess or an angelic being!

She said something like, "What's wrong with you?" I couldn't tell her. I couldn't tell myself. But I know, yes! That hit revealed the presence of the "love bug." It was that moment that I realized that I was in love with her. I'm not saying that I fell in love with her at that moment, but that powerful hit did it. She and I had been out on the turf since the 80s. In fact, both of us interrupted our times together to go do a bit. She was one of my infamous "legs" who operated out of my van. But of all the hoes I dealt with, she was the most constant. Although she didn't actually stay with me she had her closet space and special place on the bed where no one dared to lay on. There was an unofficial "hater's club" created in her honor. I caught hell from the other women because they said that whenever she came along. All the other women had to split.

An old hen would tell a new young chick that they would have to leave because she was now in the place. Look, I can say that is practically true. Some of the times, I wanted the current flock to leave especially if they didn't have any more rock. You could tell when they were out of hits or nearly out by the way they pushed their stems. Sometimes, she would want to be alone with me merely to rest. Sometimes we would play "noncontact" sex. That's when she would get buck-ball naked and lie down on the bed and play with her pretty pussy and I would beat the hell out of my little dick! There were times when I would be stroking her, but would not be able to hold it up. Then we would go into our other activity.

I would lie back, and she would give me a little head. Then I'd have her suck and nibble my tits while I masturbated.

When I would bust a nut, I would break out laughing, which is what I did. Whenever I busted a nut while with stroking in some broads' stuff or when I masturbated. Even so, there were times when we were in the room both reading and writing. Writing is something we both had in common. She was an intellectual crackhead who rather smoke crack than do something constructive with her life. Of all the times we sexed, one time stand out above all others. It was a rare time when my dick rose to maximum length and girt. I was in stroking mode.

Because she didn't like my head, I had given her a little and then I position both of us to a point where I could pound into that hairy juicy pit of passion with precision stroke, which allowed me to massage that G-spot amply so! This was our very best fuck! It was the fuck of all times. And I was in control of it. Oh! How I immortalized this dick which was at its appointed time point of orgasmic to production. And then this stupid-ass dude chose this time to pound on my door. Despite me telling him I was busy and my house lady telling him to get away from my door, he continued until he killed the feeling. As fast as I could; I got up, put on my clothes and grabbed my butcher knife and snatched opened the door. Then he got away from my door, ran out the back door at the speed of a track star. Of course, I couldn't catch him. It was years before I was able to remotely match that episode. And that was the last time I got a shot of that good pussy. But considering her track record I don't know if it's safe for me to get another shot of that. It's a fact that she truly has a killer pussy. Men from here, who dealt with her have passed away by way of heart attacks. I'm not jiving! The first was a guy who was her man for an umpteen number of years. He dropped dead at the store right after leaving my house looking for her. The guy dedicated at least fifteen hours of each day to her. If he wasn't with her he was searching her out. No Shit! He loved her beyond explanation. This guy gave her anything he could and she still treated him like dust. The other guy to die while dealing with her was a former big guy who was at time of his death became a skinny guy who looked like a refugee from a slave camp! At that time her mom warned me not to be number three. Well, thank God that I wasn't. But a friend of ours who was not in the city, left us via a heart failure. A few months later another guy who was dealing with her left this earth. Whoa! As I write this I just heard of another man has left us! I think this is a LIE!

Now, don't get me wrong I don't want to imply that she was directly responsible for the death of these men, but it's ironic that these guys were all dealing with her. Oh! Did I mention she was one of my a former "legs?"

My other legs was at this time doing wonderful. She fooled the world and got her a husband and they're doing wonderful. You know despite whatever; I truly believe God keeps a hand on some of us and steers trouble from our path. The woman did some most dangerous thing one could think of for the sake of a rock. But God has been blessing us and has been bringing us out of the pits of death. This young legs along with her mother was the dynamic duo. If there was a way to trick a person out of their stuff be it crack money, food stamp cards, or food. Those two could pull it off. I remember the day when we were parked at the corner waiting for the mother to pull off one of snatch and grab schemes on some women. As we sat in the van hitting a couple of rocks, the mother came fast trotting around the corner, hopped up in the van and ordered me to take off. Just as I started to leave these two women come around the corner with blood in their eyes and smoke coming out of their nose. Of all that they were saying, the only thing I could understand was, "Where is she? We're going to kill that bitch!"

I eased the van out of the parking lot and headed in the other direction. Fact of the matter, either direction was the other direction. As we rode down the road, I noticed that we were being followed.

She told me to keep going. Which is what I was going to do anyway. But this car followed me every twist and turn I took. They were determined to…I don't know what, but I eventually stopped on a residential street. I got out of my van and walked back to the car. Then I jumped into my role as the indignant driver. I questioned them on why were they following me. The women said a lady in my van robbed her of her money by selling her fake food stamps and that she wanted her money back. I told her that I had no idea what she was talking about but there was about to be big trouble with her by following me. And the beat goes on…

Conclusion

Well, my friend those conclude my first edition of *The Saga of A Crack Addict*. Please understand this is not the *whole* story. Oh, No! There is so much more and many more episodes I could recall, but I shared enough and to give you one idea of one man's adventure in that crack world. Yes, if this presentation stirs enough interest, I might present another volume. There's so much more I can share. However, as I write this story I'm happy to say my life has changed. Once again, I have turned my life over to my Lord and Savior Jesus Christ. No! This is not the first time I've done so.

My life had been one of those lives that God has continuously blessed. I gave my life over to Christ a long, long time ago. Yes, I've fallen down so many times, and so many times I've gotten up. But not without a fight! So many times I turned my life around and realigned myself with Satan and his cohorts. I had a good life as a sinner, or so I thought, but I was never satisfied. Like the prodigal son, I returned to my father. Yet though I loved serving God, I allowed myself to fall victim to that detrimental lifestyle.

Remember this: God is a good god! And he forgave me each and every time for my transgression.

Here I leave you with this thought:

My View of the Rock (Crack)

There are many things to set you a back,
But none can do it any quicker than crack.
Without a doubt, it has to be the devil's biggest tool,
And has been known to turn a wise man into a fool.
When you smoke it, it makes your head go 'round,

SPELLMAN BERNARD SMITH, JR. AKA SIR DOG

While it steadily grinds you into the ground.
Some dopers think it's a fabulous feast,
When, in fact, it's not fit for man or beast.
Although I tried it again and again,
I'm the first to admit it was my biggest sin.
Many of my dollars have brought a hit, or a block,
But at no time have I ever had enough of that rock.
I have tricked, robbed, and stolen, to get a hit,
Now I'm in jail facing a bit.
In time, I might again be free,
If so, when I want to get high, I'll climb a tree.
Yes, rock cocaine is the most destructive scene, and
If ever I need it, I'll get a flashlight for my beam.
For a hit, block: kibble-or-bit, less or more.
I've seen a debutant turned into a whore.
The rock will have you paranoid and uptight,
And have even a cripple man running after it all night.
There never was a whore, pimp, player, criminal, or mack as ruthless, strong, cold-blooded, or cold as crack.
If you're one of those who hasn't given it a try,
Please! Heed my advice and let it pass you bye-bye!

About the Author

In 1938, Spellman Smith was born a colored baby boy in Norfolk County, Virginia. He grew up as a Negro developed into an Afro-American and became a black man. He woke up one morning as an African American. Suddenly, he became a person of color. Will the act of re-identification ever end? Life of crime began in 1952, at the tender age of fourteen. For the next sixty years, he delved in a life of crime. For more than thirty years, he lived in one prison after another. He was one of those guys who never thought that they would be caught, despite the fact that getting caught is what always happen in HIS life.

Printed in the USA
CPSIA information can be obtained
at www.ICGtesting.com
LVHW040040291023
762449LV00002B/538

9 781684 565061